Marco's Run

Marco's Run

Wesley Cartier

Illustrated by Reynold Ruffins

Green Light Readers
Harcourt, Inc.

Orlando   Austin   New York   San Diego   Toronto   London

It's time for a run in the park.

As I run, I think, I must be fast.
I wish I could run like . . .

. . . a rabbit!

A rabbit hops through the grass.
He's kicking with his long back legs.
Off he goes.

I run like that rabbit. I hop and kick.

Then I think, I must be fast.
I wish I could run like . . .

. . . a bobcat!

A bobcat runs on the forest path.
She darts off in a flash to hunt.

I run like that bobcat. I rush down
the park path.

Then I think, I must be very fast.
I wish I could run like . . .

. . . a horse!

A horse starts with a trot. Then, all of a sudden, she takes off like the wind!

I run like that horse. The wind
swishes past me.

Then I think, I must be the fastest of all.
I wish I could run like . . .

. . . a cheetah!

A swift cheetah flashes by.
No one can catch him!

I run like that cheetah.

Then, I am huffing and puffing! I can't run anymore. Now I wish I were . . .

. . . back home.

I huff and puff and
sit down with a *thump*.

Then I think . . .

NOW I NEED A REST!

Animal Relay Races

**Marco pretends to be a rabbit, a bobcat, a horse, and a cheetah.
Now you and your friends can act like all these animals in a relay race!**

1. Line up in teams of four people.

2. The first person hops like a rabbit to the finish line and back.

3. The second person crawls like a bobcat.

4. The third person trots like a horse.

5. The fourth person runs like a cheetah.

**When everyone is finished,
you can REST just like Marco!**

ANIMAL MASKS

Make a mask of your favorite animal!

Popsicle stick

crayons or markers

scissors

WHAT YOU'LL NEED

paper plate

colored paper

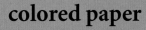

tape

1. Draw the animal face on a paper plate. Use the colored paper to make ears, whiskers, and a nose.

2. Cut out holes for the eyes.

3. Tape a Popsicle stick to your mask.

4. Wear your mask. Tell a friend what you know about your animal.

Meet the Illustrator

Reynold Ruffins loves to draw. He says, "Drawing can be a great adventure!" Drawing gives him the chance to show things that no one has ever thought of. "I like to show that pictures can tell a story just the way words do," he says.

Reynold Ruffins

www.hmhco.com

First Green Light Readers edition 2001
Green Light Readers is a trademark of Harcourt, Inc., registered in the United States of America and/or other jurisdictions.

The Library of Congress has cataloged an earlier edition as follows:
Cartier, Wesley.
Marco's run/by Wesley Cartier; illustrated by Reynold Ruffins.
p. cm.
"Green Light Readers."
Summary: A boy runs so fast that he imagines himself to be a rabbit, a bobcat, a horse, and a cheetah.
[1. Running—Fiction. 2. Speed—Fiction. 3. Imagination—Fiction.
4. Animals—Fiction.] I. Ruffins, Reynold, ill. II. Title. III. Green Light reader.
PZ7.C2485Mar 2001
[E]—dc21 00-9727
ISBN 0-15-204868-5
ISBN 0-15-204828-6 (pb)

SCP 10 9 8 7
4500523640

Ages 5–7
Grades: 1–2
Guided Reading Level: G–H
Reading Recovery Level: 14–15

Green Light Readers
For the reader who's ready to GO!

"A must-have for any family with a beginning reader."—*Boston Sunday Herald*

"You can't go wrong with adding several copies of these terrific books to your beginning-to-read collection."—*School Library Journal*

"A winner for the beginner."—*Booklist*

Five Tips to Help Your Child Become a Great Reader

1. Get involved. Reading aloud to and with your child is just as important as encouraging your child to read independently.

2. Be curious. Ask questions about what your child is reading.

3. Make reading fun. Allow your child to pick books on subjects that interest her or him.

4. Words are everywhere—not just in books. Practice reading signs, packages, and cereal boxes with your child.

5. Set a good example. Make sure your child sees YOU reading.

Why Green Light Readers Is the Best Series for Your New Reader

● Created exclusively for beginning readers by some of the biggest and brightest names in children's books

● Reinforces the reading skills your child is learning in school

● Encourages children to read—and finish—books by themselves

● Offers extra enrichment through fun, age-appropriate activities unique to each story

● Incorporates characteristics of the Reading Recovery program used by educators

● Developed with Harcourt School Publishers and credentialed educational consultants